TWIST OF FATE

THE MIRACLE COLT AND HIS FRIENDS

To Nicholas —
Have lots of fun
riding horses — hope all
your trails end in
happily ever after —
Chris Stuckenschneider

CHRIS STUCKENSCHNEIDER

PAINTINGS BY KEVIN BELFORD

Out of the darkness came light.

On September 27, 2006, a tractor-trailer crashed on Interstate 44 in rural Missouri. Forty-two horses were onboard, headed for a meatpacking plant in Illinois. The truck landed on its side, trapping the animals.
   In the inky-black night, volunteers worked side by side to save the animals. Twenty-five horses and a hinny were rescued. Many of the animals were taken to Longmeadow Rescue Ranch, a farm animal rehabilitation facility.

This is the story of Twist of Fate, "the miracle colt" of Longmeadow Rescue Ranch. Twister was born on April 18, 2007, seven months after the accident. The miracle of Twister is that his mother, Mama, was pregnant with him at the time of the accident.

Twist of Fate tells the story of the fateful night of the accident and the hope that Twister's birth inspired. Meet some of Twister and Mama's friends—Stan, Bazonka Donk, Frankie Blue Eyes, D.D., and Willy—and learn how their survival and recovery prove that hope can be just around the bend.

The country road bumps along
through woods thick with trees.
    The lane ends at Longmeadow Rescue Ranch.

In the valley, white barns and board fences
sit alongside green pastures
sprinkled with wildflowers.

There are lots of animals
at the ranch—
cows, chickens, ducks,
and even an emu.

Let me introduce you to
some of my barn buddies.

There's Mama Llama,
with her toothy grin
and movie-star lashes;

Snortin' Norton,
a 1,000-pound pig
that's hog wild
about food;

and Crackers,
a pygmy goat
with a waddle
at her throat.

BAZONKA DONK

STAN

I have horse pals too!
Stan, Bazonka Donk,
Frankie Blue Eyes,
D.D., and Willy.

FRANKIE
BLUE EYES

D. D.

WILLY

They came to the ranch
with Mama.
You will hear about them,
but first let me tell you
my story.

I was born at Longmeadow.
My entry into the world caused a celebration
across the nation.
Television crews and newspaper
reporters rushed to the ranch.

Stan the Thoroughbred was the biggest horse on the trailer. He measures seventeen hands and towers over the other horses in the barn. Though Stan is twenty-one years old, he has the pep of a spring colt.

Stan is the only accident survivor with history that can be traced. Thoroughbreds with racing potential are tattooed on the inside of their lip. Stan's tattoo helped the ranch staff track information about his past. Once, Stan had a royal title—he was Prince Conley from Lexington, Kentucky, a state where horseracing is king. Stan never got the chance to race.

He was sold, and the rest of Stan's history is a question mark with a tail longer than an Arabian's. Stan never wore a horseshoe bower of flowers in the winner's circle, but he has won everyone's heart at Longmeadow.

Every birth is
a miracle,
but mine was
front-page news.

MIRACLE COLT BORN

MOTHER HAD SURVIVED HIGHWAY ACCIDENT

Bazonka Donk was on the truck when it crashed. Rescuers couldn't get to him right away, but Donk was calm. He didn't panic even though his legs were caught.

Donk is a hinny. He has a horse for a dad and a donkey for a mom. And that's no hee-haw! Donk is copper red with a mane and tail to match. He has long ears and an amazing talent. Donk can bray like a donkey and neigh like a horse. That makes him bilingual.

No one knows much about Donk's life before the accident. But the ranch staff thinks Donk was a pack animal, a Western dude who carried supplies for people going to remote places to hunt and fish. He has a patch of white hair on his back that may have come from a pack rubbing against his coat. One thing's for sure, Donk has never had a rider on his back. The very thought makes him bristle like a porcupine.

Reporters had come to the ranch before to write about Mama, twenty-four other horses, and a hinny.

My horse pals had been rescued
after a tractor-trailer accident on the highway.

The truck was passing through Missouri
when it lost control on a turn.
With a crash, it landed on its side.

What a tragedy it must have been!
Mama told me all about it.

In the starless night,
teary-eyed rescuers released the
injured horses from the wreck.

When the sun rose, and a new day began,
Mama was safe.

She was happy so many other
horses were okay too.

Frankie Blue Eyes wasn't banged up too much in the accident, but she was thin and stressed. Already skinny, Frankie didn't want to eat at Longmeadow. She dropped another 200 pounds and earned the nickname, "Nervous Nellie." Soon, the peace at the ranch worked its magic. Then another great thing happened. Frankie was adopted. The mare now lives at Crazy Acres with Lori, a woman who helped with the rescue.

Lori works with MERS, the Missouri Emergency Response Service. MERS volunteers help large animals in trouble. Frankie is the organization's mascot. She goes to events to demonstrate how the group uses a sling to lift animals to safety. It's special that Frankie is helping other animals just like she was helped.

Mama and her pals
were taken to Longmeadow
and to other places where
animal doctors could care for them.

Three mares were going to have babies.
But I was the "miracle colt," the only one that was born.

Late one evening,
Bazonka Donk was
a hootin' and a hollerin'.
Earlene, the ranch director,
peeked into Mama's stall.

And there I was—

a brown, leggy colt
with a white lightning bolt
on my face.

Now, I needed a name!

The folks at Longmeadow had a contest. People from across the nation voted. Whoa! That made me feel important.

LUCKY STAR
PHOENIX
LONGMEADOW'S SECOND CHANCE
TRIUMPH
LIGHTENING
DREAM DANCER
TRAVELER
SERENDIPITY'S ROAD RUNNER
EQUUS FORTUNA

D.D. was badly injured on the trailer and had to go to an animal hospital before coming to Longmeadow. D.D.'s body and mind were affected. The Appaloosa was afraid of her own tail.

D.D. is chocolate with dots of white on her coat, like a brownie sprinkled with powdered sugar. Brownies and cookies are sweet, but D.D. was not.

When she came to Longmeadow, the mare wanted to get too close to people. That is okay if you are a small pup, but people don't want a horse on their lap. To cure D.D. of her bad habits, she was sent to a trainer. The trainer taught D.D. with a gentle but firm voice. After going to horse school, everyone has seen a welcome change in D.D.

My name became "Twist of Fate!"

That's more of a mouthful than an ear of corn. So you're welcome to just call me "Twister."

I get a kick out of
living at Longmeadow.
When folks come
to visit the ranch,
they stop by my stall.

Willy was the last horse to be rescued from the accident. He was in the back of the trailer and lay for hours with other horses on top of him. When rescuers finally reached him, they thought it was too late. But suddenly Willy blinked one big, brown eye. Hooray!

Because the little Appaloosa had such a strong will to live, an animal doctor at the accident site named him Willy.

The courageous survivor is now part of Longmeadow's family. Willy is happy to be a Barn Buddy, like Mama, Twist of Fate, Snortin' Norton, and some of the other animals at the ranch. Willy likes to stick his head out of his stall and get a friendly pat on the head from visitors who come to Longmeadow.

I'm a star attraction and the ranch pet.
But then all of us at Longmeadow are stars.

The staff cares for us
and makes us feel special.

With their magic touch,
they turn tragic tales
into stories that end
with "happily ever after."

Our class just finished reading Twist of Fate: The Miracle Colt and His Friends. I think this title is a great title for the story because Twist of Fate really is a miracle colt who meets some friends. If there was one thing I could change about the story, I would change Bazonka Zonk's name to Winnie the Hinny. Thank you for writing this book so that we could read it.

Thank You!

About the Ranch

Folks who live close to Longmeadow Rescue Ranch can meet Twist of Fate, Mama, and the other animals that call the ranch home. Students can even take field trips to the ranch, like this class from Union, Missouri, which is just down the road.

But even if you live far away, you can learn more about the animals through the Barn Buddy Program. Visit www.longmeadowrescueranch.org to see photos of Mama Llama, Snortin' Norton, and other barnyard animals that can become your friends.

You also can watch a live webcam of Twist of Fate, who is growing up and doing just great! He hopes you will stop in virtually or drop by if you are ever in the area, because this miracle colt has more stories to share! A portion of the proceeds of this book will benefit the Humane Society of Missouri, the organization that operates Longmeadow Rescue Ranch.

Reedy Press
PO Box 5131
St. Louis, MO 63139

No part of this publication may be reproduced or transmit-
ted in any form or by any means, electronic or mechanical,
including photocopy, recording, or any information storage
and retrieval system, without permission in writing from the
publisher.

Permissions may be sought directly from Reedy Press at the
above mailing address or via our website at www.reedypress.
com.

Library of Congress Control Number: 2009920961
ISBN: 978-1-933370-73-6

For information on all Reedy Press publications visit our
website at www.reedypress.com.

Printed in China

09 10 11 12 13   5 4 3 2 1

Dedication

Many the hands, the prayers, the care—kindhearted, giving people came together the night of the accident and the weeks and months that followed to ensure that the horses survived. These neglected animals, bound for certain death, finally received the attention and love they so sorely needed. Many gave much, and the result was miraculous.

Some girls are born loving horses. I was one of them. As a child, I had a cranky mare named Goldie and a docile stallion named Barney, who once tipped over in sleep when my cousin was shoeing him.

Writing this book is the realization of a dream, one made possible by a trio of special people.

My mother, Amy, who read the first draft, gave me the loving push I needed, and patiently read countless revisions.

My friend and editor, Dawn, who offered honest feedback and encouragement, and joined me on the roller coaster ride of ups and downs that at times seemed laughable.

My husband, Sparky, who has never been on a horse but who has always been at my side.

Additional thanks to Jeanne Miller Wood, the photo editor at the *The Washington Missourian,* the best community newspaper ever; Josh Stevens and Matt Heidenry at Reedy Press for being the book experts they are; Earlene Cole; the staff at Long-meadow Rescue Ranch; the volunteers at Missouri Emergency Response Service; the Humane Society of Missouri; and Kathy King.